Violet Mackerel's Remarkable Recovery

ANNA BRANFORD

illustrated by
SAM WILSON

WALKER
BOOKS

Thi... nts
are ...ire
use ...is,
info ...are
inclu ...lied
on tor accuracy or replicated as they may result in injury.

First published 2010 by Walker Books Australia Pty Ltd

First published in the UK 2012 by Walker Books Ltd
87 Vauxhall Walk, London SE11 5HJ

2 4 6 8 10 9 7 5 3 1

Text © 2010 Anna Branford
Illustrations © 2012 Sam Wilson

The author and illustrator have asserted their moral rights
in accordance with the Copyright, Designs and Patents Act 1988

This book has been typeset in Bembo

Printed and bound in Great Britain by Clays Ltd, St Ives plc

British Library Cataloguing in Publication Data:
a catalogue record for this book is available from the British Library

ISBN 978-1-4063-2694-9

www.walker.co.uk

www.violetmackerel.com

To Rusty (my dad)
AB

To Jay
SW

The Purple Lozenge

Violet Mackerel has an extremely sore throat.

It feels awful to talk, terrible to swallow and horrible to eat.

Her older sister, Nicola, and her brother, Dylan, have just left for school.

Violet has been home from school all week and today Mum is taking her to see Doctor Singh.

Violet likes Doctor Singh because he asks good questions such as, "Would you like to hear your heartbeat through my stethoscope?" and "Do you want to see how my examination table goes up and down?"

Also, his name makes her slightly wonder if he might be a singing sort of doctor, especially as he doesn't mind making up a little tune like

Good morning Violet Mackerel
And how are you today?
That's quite a nasty bruise you have
But it should fade away.

—

When Violet and Mum get to the
doctor's surgery, they sit in the waiting
room. Mum knits a few rows of a soft
rosy cardigan. She is
a very good knitter.

Soon the lady at the desk says, "**VIOLET MACKEREL**", which means it is time for Violet and Mum to go and see Doctor Singh.

"How are you this morning?" he asks, feeling her forehead.

"My throat hurts," croaks Violet. "It feels as if there is a cactus in it."

Doctor Singh presses a big flat lollipop stick on her tongue.

"Say **ahhhh**," he says.

"**Ahhhh**," says Violet.

"And again," says Doctor Singh.

"**Ahhhh**," says Violet.

"Hmmm," says Doctor Singh, who has been looking down Violet's throat. "I'm afraid that's a bad case of tonsillitis."

Violet has had tonsillitis before. Lots of times. It is when the two bits at the back of your throat, which are called tonsils, swell up and feel as though you have swallowed a cactus.

"I'll give you some lozenges for now, to help with the prickles," says Doctor Singh, "but I think it would be a good idea to have your tonsils taken out."

Violet, however, does *not* think this is a good idea. She generally prefers *not* to have things taken out.

"It's a very simple operation at the hospital," explains Doctor Singh, "and you'll be asleep all the way through it.

And then you'll need a while at home afterwards, resting and eating ice-cream."

Violet quite likes the idea of resting at home and eating ice-cream. But she is not sure about the hospital part. She has never had an operation before.

"What will it be like to have no tonsils?" she asks.

"The best thing is that you won't keep getting tonsillitis," says Doctor Singh.

"Anything else?" asks Violet.

Doctor Singh thinks.

"Well, some people find that their voices change a little bit after they've had their tonsils out."

This is very interesting to Violet, who always wonders about singing when she sees Doctor Singh, even though she realizes that he is not really a singing sort of doctor.

Violet wonders what her new voice might be like. Perhaps it will be an opera-singing voice like the ones you sometimes hear on the radio. Perhaps, when Violet is singing in the bath, her voice will carry down into the garden and all the way along the street. The neighbours will say, "Who is doing that lovely **opera singing**?" and Mum will say, "Oh, that is Violet. She always sings like that since she had her tonsils out."

Violet thinks she would quite like to be an **opera singer**, not just singing in the bath but also on the radio sometimes.

"Could my voice turn into an **opera-singing voice**?" squeaks Violet.

"Well, not right away," says Doctor Singh. "Your throat will be a bit too sore for any kind of singing for a little while after your operation. But I have certainly seen some *remarkable recoveries* in my time."

Violet decides that hers will be the most *remarkable recovery* Doctor Singh has ever seen in his time.

"Until then," he says, "would you like pink throat lozenges that taste like strawberries, or purple throat lozenges that taste like grapes?"

It is an excellent question, Violet thinks.

"Purple, please," she says.

Doctor Singh pops open a packet of lozenges and gives one to Violet so it can start soothing her throat prickles right away. The purple lozenge looks like a precious crystal in her hand.

And it gives Violet an idea.

The
Perfect Violet

On the drive home
Violet's idea is slowly
growing into a theory.

It is called the
**Theory of
Giving** Small
Things

and it works like this.

If someone has a problem
and you give them
        something small,
        like a feather, or a pebble, or
        a purple lozenge, then that
small thing might have a strange
and special way of helping them.
Of course, it might help in an
ordinary way. Handkerchiefs are
helpful for runny noses, elastoplasts
        are good for grazed knees and
        purple lozenges are excellent
        when you have tonsillitis.
But the small thing might
also help in an **extraordinary**
way, and that is the
interesting part.

Violet suspects, for example, that when Vincent picks a flower for Mum, it is not just the flower, but a sort of special wish tucked somewhere inside it that makes Mum have such a nice smile. (Vincent is Mum's boyfriend. He comes to their house a lot and he quite often picks Mum a flower on the way.)

She also suspects that when Doctor Singh gave her that purple lozenge, there was, tucked inside it, a little bit of the singing part of his name, which will be very helpful for turning her everyday voice into an **opera-singing** voice.

"You're very quiet," says Mum to Violet. "Are you a bit worried about going to hospital?"

"Maybe a bit," says Violet. "Have you ever been to hospital?"

"Well," says Mum, "the last time I went to hospital was when you were being born."

"Were you nervous?"

"Maybe, but I think I was too excited to notice," says Mum

That is a bit how Violet feels too.

In a photo album at Violet's house there is a picture that was taken just after Violet was born. In it she looks a bit like a tiny pink hairy monkey wrapped in a soft blanket. Mum is very

tired and there are teardrops
on her cheeks.
But she has
the look on
her face of
birthdays and
Christmases
all at once.
It is Violet's
favourite photo.

"Did you know I was going to be
a girl called Violet?" asks Violet.

"I knew you were going to be a
girl," says Mum, "but at first no one
could think of a name for you."

"Why did you decide to call me
Violet?" asks Violet.

"Well, after you were born, the midwife gave me a perfect violet for the little vase by my bed. That's what gave me the idea."

Violet smiles.

"Would you have called me Rose if the midwife had picked you a perfect rose?"

"Maybe," says Mum.

"Would you have called me Daffodil if she had picked you a perfect daffodil?"

"Probably not," says Mum.

Violet thinks about the **Theory of Giving Small Things** and she is quite glad that the midwife gave Mum a perfect violet. A violet is a very small flower. It must have been just the right sort of small thing to help Mum when she was tired after having a baby and needed to choose a good name.

"I'm not nervous about having my tonsils out," says Violet. "Not really."

Then her throat is too prickly for any more talking.

The New Verse

A few days later,
Violet finds out another
interesting thing about
having your
tonsils out,
which is that the
proper name for it is
tonsillectomy.

The day before her
trip to hospital, the
postman comes to
Violet's house to deliver
a box of wool to Mum.
"I'm having a **tonsillectomy**
tomorrow," Violet tells him.
She wonders if he will be
slightly jealous about the
ice-cream and the change of voice.

"A **tonsillectomy**? You brave little
thing!" he says.

Then, later on, a lady comes to
the door asking Mum to sign a
petition.

"I'm having a **tonsillectomy**
tomorrow," Violet tells her.

25

"A **tonsillectomy**? Goodness me!" says the lady, clucking and tutting.

No one seems to be at all jealous. But it is quite interesting to have so much clucking and tutting and people saying "goodness me".

In the evening, Mum's boyfriend Vincent is there and he is cooking dinner for everyone. Violet looks down at the kitchen floor and sighs very deeply. She hopes Vincent will ask her what is wrong, but he is a bit deaf and anyway, there is the very loud noise of chips frying in the pan.

She sighs much more loudly.

Still nothing.

"I am having a **tonsillectomy** tomorrow," says Violet. She tries to sniffle a little bit.

"I know," says Vincent. "You get to stay in bed and eat ice-cream for a week. I'm jealous."

Violet smiles.

"I am going to have a *remarkable recovery*," she tells Vincent. "When you hear me singing in the bath, you won't even know it's me. You will have to ask Mum who is doing that lovely **opera singing** and Mum will say, 'It is Violet, and soon she will be on the radio'."

Violet has been making up a verse for a song she likes called "A Few of My Favourite Things". It is from a movie about children with a nice nanny and Violet likes making up new verses for it. Her newest verse goes like this

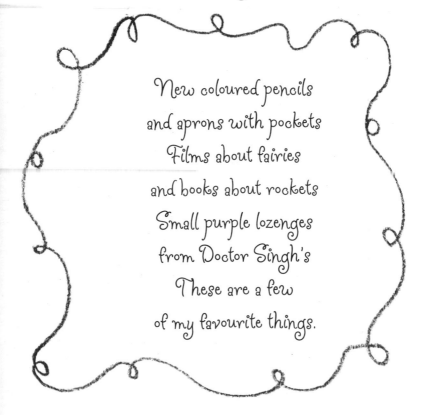

New coloured pencils
and aprons with pockets
Films about fairies
and books about rockets
Small purple lozenges
from Doctor Singh's
These are a few
of my favourite things.

Violet wishes she could sing it for Vincent and Mum but her throat is too sore.

Before she goes to sleep Violet says goodnight to her tonsils.

The Waiting Room

The next morning Violet wakes up with a strange feeling inside her. It is called butterflies, which is odd, Violet thinks, since it feels so much more like rhinoceroses.

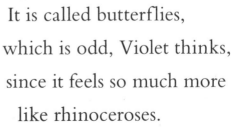

Violet can't have any breakfast because you're not supposed to eat before you have an operation. There is a nice smell of toast coming from the kitchen. The smell makes the rhinoceroses stamp around crossly inside Violet.

Mum is in her bedroom getting dressed and Violet goes in for a chat.

"I've changed my mind," says Violet. "I'm going to keep my tonsils and have some toast."

"That's a shame," says Mum. "Vincent brought so much ice-cream over that I can hardly close the door of the freezer."

"All the same flavour?" asks Violet.

"All different flavours," says Mum.

Violet thinks.

"Also," says Mum, "I was looking forward to hearing the next verse of 'A Few of My Favourite Things' being sung in your new voice."

Violet had been looking forward to that too.

So Violet takes a very deep breath and decides that maybe she will still have the **tonsillectomy** after all.

She packs a small case to take to the hospital. First she packs some ordinary things like a book and a teddy. Then she packs some other things. One is a BLUE CHINA BIRD that Vincent gave her, because she feels it may have some of Vincent's braveness tucked inside it. Vincent has been backpacking all over the world and that is the sort of braveness that is very useful when you are having a **tonsillectomy**.

Next she packs a woolly scarf that Mum made for her, because she feels it might have a sort of hug tucked into it, which might be helpful when you need to make a **remarkable recovery**.

And finally she packs a "get well soon" card that her big brother Dylan made for her. It has a picture of her singing in the opera with lots of musical notes coming out of her mouth. Dylan is a very good violin player and she feels he may have tucked some musical genius into the card. It is just the sort of thing that helps when you want to sing opera on the radio.

After Nicola and Dylan have gone to school, Mum puts a basket of wool and needles in the boot of the car so she can do some knitting while Violet is having her operation. Violet puts her bag beside it and then they are ready to go.

On the way, Violet tries to think of some new words for "A Few of My Favourite Things", but the rhinoceroses keep distracting her.

The waiting room at the hospital is bigger than at Doctor Singh's. One of the people waiting is an old lady sitting by herself. She looks as though she has been there for a very long time. Mum notices her too.

"I feel as though I've seen her somewhere before," Mum whispers to Violet.

The old lady has a green cardigan and a necklace of bright red beads and she is doing a funny thing with her hands. Her fingers, which have lots of rings on them, are all laced together and she is making her thumbs go round and round.

"Are you having a **tonsillectomy**?" Violet asks the old lady.

The old lady smiles. "No, I'm having an operation on my arm," she says.

"Do you have butterflies?" asks Violet.

"Well, they *feel* more like rhinoceroses," says the old lady.

Violet smiles.

The Old Lady

While they wait Violet asks the old lady to teach her how to do the trick with her thumbs.

It is much harder than it looks. At first
Violet's thumbs won't go round at all.
Then they start going around but they
get in a bit of a tangle.

The old lady tries
to untangle them for
her and Violet gets
the giggles. Then
the old lady gets the
giggles. There is so
much giggling that it is quite hard
for Violet to do anything else, except

wipe her eyes with
the old lady's clean
handkerchief,
which smells a little
bit like lavender.

But there is a lot of waiting to do and the old lady is a patient teacher, so eventually Violet can make her thumbs go round and round almost as well as the old lady can.

Violet wishes she had a trick to teach the old lady but she can't think of one, so instead she shows her the things in her case. The old lady especially likes the BLUE CHINA BIRD.

"It reminds me
of my garden
when I was a little
girl in the country," she says.
"There were robins in the winter and
their eggs were just that colour."

"Do you have a garden now?" asks
Violet.

"Yes," says the old lady, "though
lately my arm has been too sore to do
much gardening.

But when
I am able
to garden,
I grow
beautiful
flowers."

"After your arm operation, will you be able to grow them again?"

"I hope so," says the old lady.

"Doctor Singh says that after my **tonsillectomy** my voice will change a bit," Violet tells the lady. "Right now I have an ordinary voice, but afterwards I think it will change into an opera-singing voice."

"Really?" asks the old lady.

"Yes," says Violet. "You'll probably hear me on the radio sometime. My name is Violet Mackerel, just so you can be sure it is me. And maybe after *your* operation, your ordinary arm will turn into a **super arm**. Then you will be able to do lots of gardening and lots of other things too. When the neighbours can't get the lids off their jars, they will bring them to your house and you'll be able to do it first try."

The old lady laughs. "It would be handy to have a super arm," she says.

Violet thinks about the **Theory of Giving** Small **Things** and she wishes she had a small thing that might help to change a sore arm into a **super arm**. She asks Mum if there are any more purple lozenges.

"I don't know if you should have one right before your operation," says Mum.

"It's not for me," says Violet and Mum gives her a purple lozenge.

Violet wraps the purple lozenge up in a tissue like a present and gives it to the old lady. She explains the **Theory of Giving** small **Things** and tells her about how, tucked inside the purple lozenge, there could be a little bit of Violet's own superness.

"Thank you," says the old lady.

Then a nurse comes out and says in a loud voice, "**IRIS MACDONALD**".

"That's me," says the old lady.

"How are your rhinoceroses?" asks Violet.

"They're not too bad now actually," says the-old-lady-Iris-MacDonald,

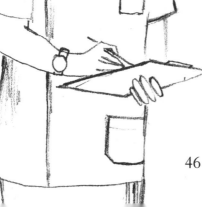

putting the purple lozenge in her cardigan pocket. "It was lovely to meet you," she says to Violet.

"It was lovely to meet you too," says Violet.

But Violet doesn't feel quite ready just to say goodbye and never see her new friend again.

"When we have both had **remarkable recoveries**, I think we should have tea together so you can hear my **opera-singing** voice and I can see your **super arm**," says Violet.

"Let's do that," says Iris MacDonald.

"Promise?" asks Violet.

"I promise," says Iris MacDonald

They wave goodbye.

Violet's rhinoceroses aren't too bad now either.

The Actual Tonsillectomy

The next time the nurse comes out, he says, "**VIOLET MACKEREL**".

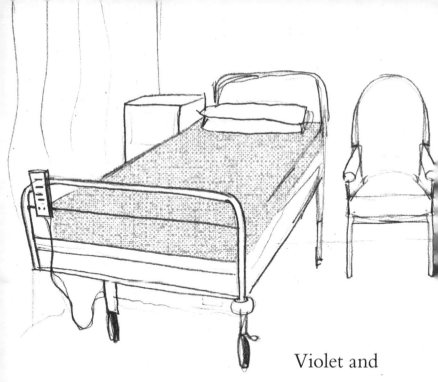

Violet and
Mum pack
up their things and follow him down
a little corridor. They meet a doctor,
and the nurse shows Violet the bed that
will be hers while she is in hospital.
The mattress is a bit thinner than her
bed at home, but it is as white as a
cloud and Violet quite likes it.

She does not at all like the part where they give her a needle and it feels like a sharp little pinch on her arm, but it is over very, very quickly and then she drifts off to sleep.

Violet sleeps right through the **tonsillectomy** and when she wakes up, still on her cloud bed, Mum is there and the **tonsillectomy** is finished. There are three whole new roses in the cardigan Mum is knitting, so Violet must have been asleep for quite a long time.

"Hello," says Mum, smiling. "How are you feeling?"

"A bit groggy," croaks Violet.

She sleeps a bit more with Mum next to her and then she wakes up again and watches Mum knitting for a while. It is a nice thing to see while you are drowsing after a **tonsillectomy**.

Soon she feels well enough to sit up and Mum has a cup of tea and Violet

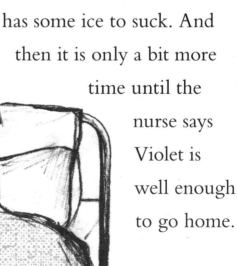

has some ice to suck. And then it is only a bit more time until the nurse says Violet is well enough to go home.

When she gets home Violet is still feeling groggy, so she goes back to bed with a hot water bottle even though it is daytime outside. Nicola, who is a very good jewellery maker, has made her a beautiful necklace. The beads have little letters of the alphabet on them and they spell out **G-E-T-W-E-L-L-S-O-O-N-V-I-O-L-E-T**. It is in a little box by Violet's bed.

Violet drifts in and out of sleep
and has strange dreams
of butterflies with
rhinoceros horns
and rhinoceroses
with butterfly wings,
and rhinocerflies and
butternoceroses with
necklaces which say "**G-E-T-W-E-L-L-S-O-O-N**". Mum and Nicola and
Dylan and Vincent
come in and say
"hello" and "how
are you feeling?",
but Violet is too
sleepy and groggy to
say too much back.

The next morning, though, she feels
a bit better. Mum has to go out to a
special knitting workshop, so Vincent
comes round to look after Violet
and they eat minty ice-cream with
pink bits and watch the movie about
the children and the nanny with the
song "A Few of My
Favourite Things".

Then Violet feels floppy again so Vincent refills her hot water bottle and they listen to some **opera music** on the radio.

"My throat feels funny and I still feel a bit groggy," whispers Violet. "Do you think that means my recovery isn't going to be very remarkable?"

"No," says Vincent. "I think even very **remarkable recoveries** probably take a few days."

"I think so too," says Violet, who is drifting off to sleep again.

When she wakes up Vincent has gone home and Mum is back from the knitting workshop. She tries to refill Violet's water bottle but Vincent has twisted the top in so tightly that she can't get it out. After a little while her face is all red from trying.

"It's no good," she says. "My arm isn't strong enough."

And then, suddenly, Violet remembers the old-lady-Iris-MacDonald.

The Totbafim Plot

"How are we going to find
Iris MacDonald?" asks
Violet, scratchily.

"Who?"

says Mum.

"The-old-lady-Iris-MacDonald *promised* we would have tea when we were better so she could hear my opera voice and I could see her **super arm**. But she doesn't have our phone number and we don't have hers, so how will we be able to have tea with her?"

Mum thinks.

"She knows my name is Violet Mackerel," says Violet, "and there aren't many other Mackerels in the phone book, so maybe she will look us up."

"She might," says Mum.

"But what if she doesn't quite remember my name?" asks Violet.

"What if she remembers Violet, but not quite Mackerel?"

"Well …" begins Mum.

"Let's phone the hospital and ask them and tell them it is an emergency," says Violet.

"I'm not sure that this is really the kind of emergency that hospitals help with," says Mum.

Mum thinks a bit more.

"Violet, it *might* be that Iris MacDonald was just a friend for the time you were in the hospital waiting room and not really the sort of friend for having tea with afterwards."

This suggestion of Mum's makes

Violet feel quite cross. Her throat is too sore from her **tonsillectomy** to have a cross voice, so instead she frowns until her eyebrows almost get in her eyes.

"Iris MacDonald is *not* that kind of friend," she says to Mum.

Violet frowns more. Frowning is not as good as a cross voice, which people have to hear whether they want to or not. People have to be looking right at you to see how hard you are frowning, and Mum is not looking.

"Please can I have my notebook?" Violet asks Mum, when her eyebrows are too tired to frown any more.

Mum brings a tray
with a bowl of frosty
forest-berry ice-cream,

a notebook and a pencil
to Violet's bedroom and
Violet starts a new page,
which is called

Thinking Outside the Box
About Finding Iris MacDonald

Thinking Outside the Box is when
you find ***extraordinary*** solutions
to problems and puzzles, because
extraordinary solutions are often better
than the ordinary sort. It is one of
Violet's favourite problem-solving
strategies.

In brackets, after

Thinking Outside the Box
About Finding Iris MacDonald

Violet writes

(The TOTBAFIM Plot)

The word TOTBAFIM is made
from the first letters of all the words
in her plot.

T hinking
O utside
T he
B ox
A bout
F inding
I ris
MacDonald

Next on the page she draws a big box and inside the box she writes her ordinary ideas, such as

> ＊ Ask everyone we know if they know a nice old lady called Iris MacDonald
>
> ＊ Ask everyone we know to ask everyone they know if they know a nice old lady called Iris MacDonald

Then outside the box she writes her extraordinary ideas, such as

Hire one of those little aeroplanes
that can write things in clouds
in the sky and write
"If your name is Iris MacDonald,
please could you phone Violet Mackerel?"

* Ask everyone we know if
they know a nice old lady
called Iris MacDonald

* Ask everyone we know to
ask everyone they know if
they know a nice old lady
called Iris MacDonald

Put an advertisement in
the Lost and Found section
of the newspaper which says,
"Lost: One old lady called
Iris MacDonald with a super arm."

They are all good ideas, Violet thinks,
especially the ones outside the box.

But it is very difficult to make any of them happen from your bed where you are still recovering from a **tonsillectomy**. That is the problem.

She thinks about Iris MacDonald somewhere out in the world recovering in her own bed and probably wondering about the girl she met in the waiting room. She might never hear Violet's opera-singing voice and Violet might never see her **super arm**. And they might never, ever get to have tea together.

The
Star Message

That night before bed, while she
is eating passionfruit ice-cream,
Violet is still feeling sad.

She asks
Dylan if he
will help her
to find Iris
MacDonald,

and he says he will put a little notice about her in his violin case. Dylan plays his violin at the market on Saturday mornings and people throw coins in his case.

Violet is not sure.

Violet also asks Nicola if she will help her to find Iris MacDonald, and Nicola says she will put up a sign on the noticeboard at school.

"I don't think Iris MacDonald will see it there," says Violet.

Violet says thank you to her brother and sister for trying, but before she goes to sleep she decides that she will ring up Vincent and see if he has any ideas.

"The **TOTBAFIM** Plot didn't work," Violet tells him.

"The **TOTBAFIM** Plot?" says Vincent, thoughtfully.

"What's that?"

"It was the plan to help me find Iris MacDonald who I met in the hospital waiting room."

"If it *had* worked and you *had* found her, what would you have said?" asks Vincent.

Violet thinks.

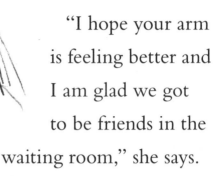

"I hope your arm
is feeling better and
I am glad we got
to be friends in the
waiting room," she says.

Violet is surprised that it isn't a
message about her **opera-singing**
voice and the **super arm**, or even the
afternoon tea. Sometimes you don't
even know what you think until
someone asks you a question like that.

"When you are a backpacker like
me," says Vincent, "you meet lots and
lots of special people just once and
never get to see them again. So what I
do, sometimes, is send messages to the
stars for them."

"Do they get your messages?" asks Violet, whose scratchy throat is getting too tired for much more talking.

"I don't know," says Vincent. "But maybe they feel something special when they look at the stars that night."

It is a good idea, Violet thinks.

She says goodnight to Vincent, because her throat is too scratchy to talk any more, and she looks out at the stars through her bedroom window. She rests her hands on the windowsill and circles her thumbs in the way of the-old-lady-Iris-MacDonald.

"This is a message for Iris MacDonald," whispers Violet to the stars as her thumbs go round and round.

Thank you for being my friend in the waiting room and I hope your arm is getting better. Even very remarkable recoveries can take a few days, so don't worry if your arm is not super yet. Lots of love from Violet Mackerel. (There are not many Mackerels in the phone book so if you want to look me up you still can.)

That night in bed, before she goes
to sleep, Violet composes a verse of
"A Few of My Favourite Things"
especially in honour of Iris MacDonald.

After that she feels a bit better.

The Gardening Channel

While she is getting better, Violet spends quite a lot of time listening to the radio, which Vincent has put on the small table next to her bed. Best of all she likes listening to opera music.

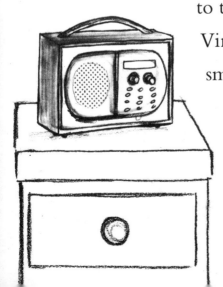

Even though her voice is getting better at talking, it has mostly been too scratchy to think much about singing. But Violet still likes imagining the radio host saying, "And that was Violet Mackerel, who never sang like that before her **tonsillectomy**."

This morning there is no opera music on any of the radio stations, so Violet decides that she will listen to the gardening channel, since somebody has rung in to ask a question about violets.

"The leaves on my violets have dead spots. I've tried everything but it just keeps on happening," says the caller.

"Hmmm," says the host of the gardening channel. "I'm afraid I don't know much about growing violets, but if any of our listeners have any ideas, we'd love to hear from you."

Violet wishes she knew the answer to the problem. She would quite like to ring up and talk on the radio. She listens to a few more questions but they're not about violets so they're not so interesting.

Then a lady rings up who says she has an answer to the violet question, so Violet listens carefully again.

"It sounds like a problem with watering," says the lady. "The trick with watering violets is to do it from underneath, not from above. They much prefer to sit in water for a little while than be sprinkled and get water on their leaves."

There is something very familiar about her voice.

"Thank you for calling, you've been very helpful," says the radio host. "What was your name?"

"Iris MacDonald," says the lady.

"MUM!" yells Violet, too excited to notice that she is yelling and her throat is feeling better, "THE-OLD-LADY-IRIS-MACDONALD IS ON THE RADIO!"

Mum is not as excited as Violet. This is because she sloshed tea down her dressing-gown when she heard Violet yelling, and rushed up the stairs to see if she was being eaten by an escaped zoo animal.

The next time the radio host
gives the telephone number for the
gardening channel,
Violet writes it
down in her
notebook. Then
she picks up the
phone and dials.

"Hello," says the radio host. "Can
you answer any of our gardening
questions this morning?"

Violet thinks.

"I agree about watering the violets,"
she says. "I am a Violet and I much
prefer sitting in the bath to being
sprinkled in the shower."

"I see," says the radio host.

"But that is not why I called," says Violet. "I called because I met Iris MacDonald in the hospital waiting room when I was having my **tonsillectomy**."

It is funny for Violet to hear her own voice talking on the radio as well as down the phone.

"I see," says the radio host again, but he sounds as though he doesn't *quite* see.

"We were supposed to have tea together, so I could see her **super arm** and she could hear my **opera-singing** voice," says Violet. "I am going to be an **opera singer** on the radio," she explains.

"Well," says the radio host, "you're on the radio now.

Would you like to sing a song for Iris?"

"Yes please," says Violet.

She pauses for a moment just to make sure Iris MacDonald will have time to get nice and close to her radio.

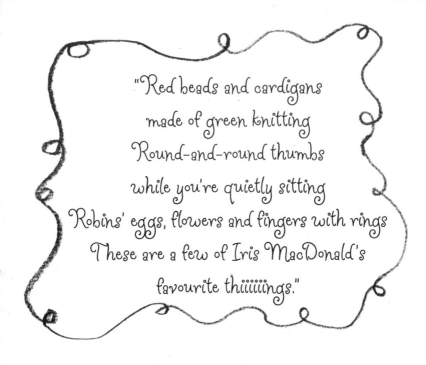

"Red beads and cardigans
made of green knitting
Round-and-round thumbs
while you're quietly sitting
Robins' eggs, flowers and fingers with rings
These are a few of Iris MacDonald's
favourite thiiiiiings."

When she sings thiiiiiings, Violet
jiggles a little bit and her voice
does sound
a lot like
an **opera**
singer.

"That was lovely," says the man. "Thank you very much for calling, Violet."

"You're welcome," says Violet.

A little while later the phone rings and it is someone from the gardening channel with a message for Violet and Mum from Iris MacDonald. The message is an invitation for tea tomorrow at eleven o'clock.

This time Violet carefully writes down all the details.

The Super Arm

Just when Violet
is thinking that
eleven o'clock
tomorrow
will never,
ever come, it
finally does.

To get to the front door of Iris MacDonald's house you have to walk through some of her garden and it is very beautiful.

There is even a violet patch, with no spots on the leaves. Mum rings the doorbell and Iris MacDonald answers it. Her arm is in a plaster cast in a sling, which makes hugs tricky, but she and Violet manage anyway.

"Thank you very much for inviting us," says Mum.

"Thank you for coming," says Iris MacDonald. "I was so disappointed when I realized we'd parted without exchanging phone numbers. I couldn't think how I was going to keep my promise!"

Violet does not say "I told you so", but she does raise her eyebrows just a little bit at Mum.

Iris MacDonald has a cake with
lemon icing and a pot of tea and there
are rosy teacups on saucers. Violet and
Mum help her to carry it all out from
the kitchen as it is difficult to carry lots
of things at once if you are only using
one arm. They sit down in the living
room and Violet looks at all the little
ornaments on the shelves and wonders
if they are all small gifts with hidden
helpfulness tucked inside them.

"Now," says
Iris MacDonald
when she has
had some cake.
"Even though
I am older than
seventy, I have never had
a song written for me before.
Could I hear that lovely verse again?"

"Yes," says Violet, and she sings
"A Few of Iris MacDonald's Favourite
Things", jiggling on the final *thiiiiiings*
like a real **opera singer**.

"I love it," says Iris MacDonald.
"And I can't believe how many of
my favourite things you managed to
squeeze in."

Violet smiles.

"What about your arm?" she asks.
"Is it starting to feel super yet?"

"Not really," says Iris MacDonald.
"I still keep your purple lozenge in my
pocket, just in case. But if you like,
I will tell you and your mum a secret
about my arm."

Violet and Mum
listen very carefully,
because they both
quite like secrets.

"The real truth,"
whispers Iris
MacDonald,
"is that both
of my arms are

already pretty special. For all of my working life I have been a midwife, so I have helped hundreds and hundreds and *hundreds* of mothers to give birth. That means my arms have been the first arms to hold hundreds and hundreds and *hundreds* of new babies. In fact, some of the babies I've helped to deliver have grown up and come back so I can help them deliver *their* babies."

Violet is just thinking what a good secret it is when Mum does a cough like a small explosion in her cup of tea.

"I knew I'd seen you somewhere before," squeaks Mum. "You were my midwife when I gave birth to Violet! We chose her name because of the perfect violet you gave me afterwards."

The-old-lady-Iris-MacDonald's face has the smile of someone who is not very old at all.

"I often took flowers from my garden to give to the new mothers," she says.

Violet can hardly believe it.

"I have never met anyone with arms like yours before," she says.

"And I have *never* met a real **opera singer** who sings on the radio before," says Iris MacDonald.

Before Violet goes home, Iris
MacDonald gives her a little envelope
and in it is a card which says

Dear Violet,
Congratulations on your
remarkable recovery,

With love from
Iris MacDonald xxx

And tucked inside it is another perfect violet.

Don't forget to try out

Violet's Theory of Giving Small Things

Find lots of

Violet Mackerel

things to make and do at:

www.violetmackerel.com

Another Violet Mackerel story:

Violet thinks she would
QUITE LIKE to own the blue china
bird at the Saturday market.

This is not just a SILLY WISH.

It is instead the start of a
VERY IMPORTANT idea.

But what she needs is a PLOT.

A BRILLIANT plot...

ANNA BRANFORD was born on the Isle of Man, but spent her childhood in Sudan, Papua New Guinea and Australia. Once, when she was very itchy with the chicken pox, her dad read her *The Very Hungry Caterpillar* thirty times in a row.

Anna lectures in Sociology at Victoria University, Australia, and spends her evenings writing children's stories, kept company by a furry black cat called Florence. She also makes dolls using recycled fabric and materials.

SAM WILSON graduated from Kingston University in 1999 and has since been working on lots of grown-up books. The Violet Mackerel books are the first titles she has illustrated for children. She says, "I have always wanted to illustrate for children, it has been such fun drawing Violet, she is a gorgeous character with such an adventurous spirit." Sam lives in the countryside with her husband, two children, a black Lab called Jess and several chickens.